PUFFIN BOOKS

Published by the Penguin Group

Penguin Putnam Books for Young Readers,

345 Hudson Street, New York, New York 10014, U.S.A.

Penguin Books Ltd, 80 Strand, London WC2R ORL, England

Penguin Books Australia Ltd, Ringwood, Victoria, Australia

Penguin Books Canada Ltd, 10 Alcorn Avenue, Toronto, Ontario, Canada M4V 3B2

Penguin Books (N.Z.) Ltd, 182-190 Wairau Road, Auckland 10, New Zealand

Penguin Books Ltd, Registered Offices: Harmondsworth, Middlesex, England

Published in the United States of America by Puffin Books,

a division of Penguin Putnam Books for Young Readers, 2002

Published simultaneously by Dutton Children's Books

1 3 5 7 9 10 8 6 4 2

TM & © 2002 DreamWorks LLC

Text by Kathleen Duey

All rights reserved

Puffin Books ISBN 0-14-230115-9

Printed in the United States of America

The characters and story in this book were inspired by the
DreamWorks film *Spirit: Stallion of the Cimarron.*

Chapter One

*T*hey say the history of the West was written
from the saddle of a horse. But it's never
been told from the heart of one. Not until now.

I was born here, in the place that men would
come to call the Old West. But to my kind, the
land was ageless. It had no beginning and no
end—no boundary between earth and sky.

Spirit's homeland was a perfect place for a wild
colt to be born. There were wide blue skies and deep
red-rock canyons. Tall pines grew in the mountains.
It was beautiful.
Deep, clear rivers ran through the rich valleys.

Eagles swooped through the skies, their whistling cries carrying for miles on the wind.

And the grasslands were *endless*.

Spirit was born in the springtime. His mother labored hard, lying near the herd, half hidden in the tall grass. Spirit came into the world, then lay still a moment, resting.

His mother, Esperanza, waited until he opened his eyes. Then she nudged him gently. He blinked, taking in his first sight of his homeland—and his mother.

Both were wonderful things to see. Spirit glimpsed the deep blue of the sky and the swaying grass, then focused on his mother's face.

Esperanza was a palomino, with a silken white mane and tail and a wide white blaze on her face. Her coat shone gold in the sun.

The first thing Spirit felt was his mother's warm touch. He looked into her eyes and saw both love and pride. He tilted his head and took a deep breath. Then he concentrated on untangling his long legs as he struggled to stand up.

Like all colts, Spirit was awkward and clumsy at first.

His legs felt too long and too skinny.

He wobbled as he walked, staring at *everything*.

There were other horses—lots of them. This was his herd, his family. A breeze ruffled his short, curly tail and he shivered with excitement. There was so much to explore.

Esperanza led off very slowly, stopping when he leaped forward and tumbled into the grass. He hit hard and rolled over. Esperanza waited patiently for him to struggle upright again. Spirit inhaled the glorious smell of fresh green grass, glanced at the sky, and tried walking again. This time he managed not to fall. His clumsiness faded with every step. As his mother walked slowly toward the herd, he managed to keep up.

By the time Spirit was three days old he could gallop. When he was two weeks old, he began to race with the other colts. He usually won—even against the yearlings.

Spirit spent his first summer growing and learning. He bucked and reared, and practiced jumping over rocks and fallen logs.

He met some of the herd's neighbors—deer and raccoons and foxes—and he saw the eagle flying high overhead. He watched it floating through the endless sky, spiraling, completely *free*. Its cry seemed to pierce his heart.

The Cimarron herd, Spirit learned, shared their homeland with many other creatures. And there was plenty of room for all of them.

Esperanza taught him which of the creatures were friends and which ones could be enemies. He wrinkled his muzzle the first time he scented a mountain lion. Esperanza nudged him back into the protective herd, then led them all away from the lion's scent.

The next time Spirit smelled the scent of a big cat, he began to move away from it even before his mother did. She looked at him proudly. He learned fast.

Spirit's first year was full of fun and beauty. He loved summer with its deep grass and bright meadow flowers. When summer passed and autumn began, he galloped through piles of red and gold leaves, scattering them as he raced with his friends.

Soon, deer began passing through his homeland on their way down to the valleys for winter. Spirit loved to watch them run, their cloven hooves barely touching the ground.

When winter finally came, Spirit found that he liked it as much as the other seasons. By the time the first snows fell, the brash young horse was swift and strong. When the herd galloped together, their hearts and spirits high, he could keep up with ease.

One morning Spirit was running with the rest of the herd. He loved the sound they made, their hoofbeats muffled by the deep snow—like distant thunder rolling across the land.

The cold air and the flying snow made Spirit's heart sing. He pounded along with the others, then noticed a clear slope up ahead. He veered off from the herd and raced up the ridge, glancing back at the others galloping below.

The snow was deep and soft as he charged through it, running parallel with the herd and determined not to fall behind. Then the slope of the land changed and he found himself starting downward.

The other side of the ridge was steeper. Far steeper!

Spirit skidded. For an instant he thought he might fall, then he caught his balance. His heart thudding, he leaped into a long slide. Far below, the herd had stopped. He saw some of them looking uphill and tossing their manes, watching him.

Plunging downhill, Spirit threw his weight backward and shoved his forelegs out, sledding down the mountainside. All around him, the snow sprayed outward, then began to roll down the slope, a colt-sized avalanche.

He rode the sliding snow, bumping over a rise, then skidding on again.

Finally, where the ground leveled out, he slid sideways, sending up a plume of powdery snow that landed on his mother and the horses standing near her.

Esperanza stood for a moment, her face and mane coated in white.

The others stared at him, both startled and irritated.

Esperanza shook the snow off and looked at her son. She sighed. One thing was clear. He wasn't going to be an ordinary stallion. He was already braver and bolder than most of the grown horses.

Spirit stood tall and straight, his neck arched proudly. He hadn't meant to slide down the mountainside—but it had been fun and exciting. Spirit pranced back into the herd and knew the other colts were glancing at him enviously, wishing they had been the adventurous ones. But they hadn't. He had.

Not long after Spirit had proved that a colt could turn a mountainside into a snowslide, the weather warmed up for a few days. Mornings and nights were still cold, but the midday sun shone strongly enough to start melting the snow in the treetops.

As it melted, water dripped downward. But every evening, the drips began to freeze and the long nights hardened them into clear ice again. Within a week, long, clear icicles had formed on the branches.

Every time it warmed up, the icicles dripped ice-cold water as pure and sweet as any spring. One sunny day the herd gathered beneath the trees to catch the icy drips of water on their tongues.

Suddenly, Spirit decided to taste the ice itself. Impulsively, he reared, reaching upward. But the icicles were too high. Disappointed, he tried again. He stretched his neck, trying hard to reach. Then he noticed a sparkling cluster clinging to a lower branch. Delighted, he reached up and opened his mouth wide, closing it around a huge icicle.

For one wonderful instant the ice melted against his tongue, but then he felt it re-freeze—and his tongue was stuck!

Spirit tried to pull free, shaking his head, but the ice had frozen itself firmly onto his tongue. Finally, shaking his head hard, he managed to break the icicle off the branch.

Startled and off balance, Spirit sank back down onto all four hooves, feeling the terrible coldness on his sensitive tongue. Knowing that all the other horses would soon notice the silly thing he had done, he lifted his head.

Prancing as though he were proud of the icicle stuck painfully in his mouth, Spirit passed the others. He arched his neck and acted as though he had planned the whole thing.

Spirit couldn't tell if the other colts believed it or not, but he held his head high and kept going until he was out of sight.

Only then did he slowly work the icicle free and spit it out. His tongue was sore for several days. Spirit admired icicles from a distance after that!

All winter long, the herd came to the lake to drink. The older horses would wade into the shallows to break the ice if the water had frozen overnight. Once the ice was shattered, the colts and fillies could come and go, drinking when they pleased.

One day, Spirit and three other colts his age came to the lake together on a cold morning. As usual, Spirit led the way.

Together, the colts waded into the icy water, leaping and playing, then settled down and began to drink. Spirit lowered his muzzle into the ice-cold water, enjoying the sweet taste. Then he paused, blinking.

There was a strange sound—a rumbling in the earth. The surface of the water began to vibrate.

Spirit jerked his head up. The other colts were twisting around, racing back toward the herd. Spirit stood his ground, unsure whether or not the sound was dangerous. When it stopped, he relaxed and lowered his head to drink again.

Suddenly, a motion caught his eye and he tucked his head between his front legs, staring at the shoreline behind him.

What he saw astonished him and he whirled around to face a wall of huge woolly beasts.

Buffalo! They were as tall as trees—or so it seemed to Spirit. The biggest bull was staring down at him sternly.

Trembling a little, but determined not to let it show, Spirit lifted his head and looked straight into the eyes of the huge animal.

The bull took a deep breath and let out a roaring bellow that nearly knocked Spirit down.

Spirit wanted to run for the safety of the herd—
but he didn't. Many animals drank from this lake.
The Cimarron herd used it all winter long. He had
a perfect right to be here.

Determined not to let the huge animal scare
him, Spirit gathered his courage and stretched out
his neck, whinnying back at it in his high, clear
colt's voice.

The enormous buffalo blinked, amazed and
amused at the bravery of this half-grown horse.
Now Spirit reared playfully, stretching upward. For
an instant he rested his forehooves on the buffalo's
broad muzzle to steady himself. Then he dropped
back down the ground.

The bull lowered his head a little, politely re-
turning Spirit's friendly greeting. The buffalo began
to spread out, wading into the shallow water to
drink.

Esperanza whinnied from the bank, beckoning
for Spirit to come back to the herd. He gazed for
another second at the magnificent buffalo, then cantered away.

As he topped the ridge, Spirit stopped to rear and strike at the air, just like a grown stallion claiming his homeland would have done. That was what he wanted one day. He wanted to be the stallion of the Cimarron herd, just as his father, Strider, had been before him.

Chapter Two

And so I grew from a colt to stallion, as wild and reckless as the thunder over the land. I raced with the eagle and soared with the wind. Flying? There were times I believed I could.

This was my homeland. As far as I could see, there was no end to my world and to who I would always be.

Like my father before me, I became the leader of the Cimarron herd. And with that honor...came responsibility.

As winter passed, Spirit grew taller and stronger. When spring came again, he began to stand watch, circling the herd at times, to make sure no enemies were near.

One day, he stood alone on a ridge above the grazing herd, enjoying the sunshine on his back. He had made his way around the herd—there was no danger in the wind.

Spirit heard the clear, high whistle of the eagle's call.

He looked up. The magnificent bird was swooping lower, crying out again as though challenging him to a race. None of the other horses could even come close to beating him and the challenge caught his heart.

Assured that the herd was safe, Spirit lunged into a gallop, his hooves striking the hard ground, his mane flying.

It felt wonderful to gallop as he had as a colt, flat out and thinking only about winning the race.

But following the eagle's course was not easy. Spirit leaped fallen logs, plunged downhill, then lunged upslope again chasing the gliding bird.

Hooves clattering on the ground, his body stretched out for speed. Spirit felt young and strong—and free. As he galloped, the wind lifting his mane and tail to stream out behind him, Spirit watched the eagle swoop, sliding in an arc through the blue sky. Her tail feathers spread wide, she turned as easily as the wind.

Spirit galloped faster, keeping up with the eagle as she soared high once more, then swooped again. He glanced to make sure the herd was grazing quietly below, that there was no danger nearby. Then he concentrated on the race, pounding across the homeland he loved.

Abruptly, the eagle dropped down. She flew low, almost within Spirit's reach as he galloped. Together they swept forward, the eagles wings beating in time with the thundering of Spirit's flashing hooves.

Spirit loved to run like this over the open land. His breath seemed to come and go in the rhythm of his gallop, of the eagle's wings, of the earth itself.

The green grass streamed past beneath his

hooves. The sharp-peaked mountains on the horizon seemed to watch him and the eagle. Spirit stretched out, racing with all his speed, all his strength, all his joy in his own freedom.

Then, thundering to the top of the rise, he suddenly faced a sheer drop-off. He reared, pivoting to keep from going over the precipice.

The eagle banked into a steep turn and faced Spirit as he reared, her wings outspread. For a moment they studied each other, and Spirit knew she understood him—and that he understood her. The magnificent bird cried out before she slid sideways in the air once more, gliding onward, sailing out over the valley.

For a long moment Spirit stood still, letting the wind carry the cries of the eagle back to him as she sailed on through the endless sky. Spirit watched her go, his heart flying with her, free and brave.

The stallion of any herd has to be alert for danger all the time. Spirit knew this—he had always known it. The herd was his responsibility and he did his best to protect it. His mother helped when she could. But sometimes he had to react quickly on his own.

Even with Spirit alert and wary, enemies sometimes managed to come close. The day Spirit raced the eagle, a cougar was slinking silently toward the herd, staying upwind so that the horses could not scent it.

Two foals were playing in the meadow above the grazing herd. By the time Spirit cantered back toward them and saw the huge, muscular cat, it was so close that it was impossible to stop its attack.

The colts were terrified.

They ran, squealing, toward their mothers.

Furious that this predator had gotten so close while he had raced carelessly with the eagle, Spirit lunged after the cougar, gaining ground fast.

Galloping in terror, one colt stumbled and fell. The cougar sprang toward it, snarling.

Spirit charged forward, leaping between the huge cat and the helpless colt at the last second.

The cougar snarled and began to circle him. Its

scent, rank and terrifying, filled Spirit's nostrils. He glanced down the slope to see Esperanza gathering the herd together, making sure the colts were close.

Spirit stared at the cat again. It was up to him to protect the mares and colts now. He braced himself just as the cat lunged forward.

Rearing, Spirit struck at the cat's face with his forehooves. It flinched backward and snarled again, showing its wicked, curved teeth. Spirit whirled and kicked high, forcing it back again.

The cat sprang without warning, leaping onto Spirit's back.

Its claws were long and sharp and Spirit staggered beneath its weight and the sudden pain.

Spirit was deeply afraid. His instincts told him that the cat could bite his neck from this position, and that the wound might cripple him.

Heaving his weight to one side, Spirit tried to throw the big cat off his back. But it didn't fall. It only tightened its powerful claws into his skin.

Desperate, Spirit bucked and whirled, then gathered himself and leaped forward, tucking his head between his forelegs. He vaulted into a dangerous fall few horses would attempt, rolling head over heels, crashing onto his back.

The cat screamed and released its hold, rolling onto the grass. Then it lay still, stunned.

Spirit reared, ready to pound the big cat with his forehooves. As his legs crashed to the ground, the cougar scrambled to get away. Spirit gave chase. He drove the cougar for a long way before he turned back.

Rousing the herd into a gallop, Spirit ran with them, feeling the power in the thunder of their hooves. The wind rinsed the stink of the cougar from his coat. Following the curve of the valley, Spirit kept the horses at a flat-out gallop for miles.

Then, choosing a place where the wind did not carry any scent of danger, Spirit slowed. As the herd settled into grazing again, he swerved and charged up a slope to a treeless bluff overlooking the valley. At the top, he stopped.

From that height, he could see the horizon in every direction.

He could see the blue mountains beyond the wide valley.

No enemies could sneak close here.

The herd was safe.

As the sun lowered, Spirit went back down to the valley floor. He passed through the herd slowly, touching each of the horses lightly with his muzzle, bidding them good night.

No cougar would ever catch him playing like that again and he wanted them all to know it. He wanted all the mares—and especially the colts—to know that he would be even more careful from now on. They could sleep safely here.

A few nights later, the herd was relaxed again, the colts playing and delaying bedtime as long as they could. As Spirit passed through the herd, the two colts he had saved from the cougar bounded off together, as frisky as ever.

They bumped into one mare, then startled another. Spirit gave them a stern look and they quieted. But when he glanced back at them, their eyes were bright and their ears were pricked forward. He knew they would probably start playing again before they gave in and slept.

Spirit let out a long breath, remembering when he had been the most rambunctious colt of them all. It had been a wonderful time in his life, but it was over. He had to consider the safety and welfare of all the horses now. They depended on him to guide them and protect them. Knowing that made him feel strong and proud.

Esperanza saw him pass and joined him. Her fine white mane and tail stood out in the dusky light and Spirit looked at her sidelong.

He was fortunate to have a mother who was strong and brave—and so beautiful. She had led the herd for a long time while he was growing up. Now it was his turn to protect her—to protect all of them.

Esperanza glanced at Spirit and he could see the love and pride in her eyes. Then she turned off and went to find her place among the herd. Spirit knew she would calm the colts and that her presence always made the herd feel safer.

Spirit climbed a knoll that gave him a good view of the valley. The evening breeze was picking up. He climbed slowly, enjoying the coolness of the night and the first chirping calls of the crickets.

Standing tall, Spirit positioned himself carefully on the high ground, facing into the wind.

The darkness was thickening and a few stars were coming out. The herd in the valley below moved and shifted, each one finding a comfortable place to sleep.

The sound of small hooves told him that the colts were still awake.

A soft neigh from Esperanza told him that his mother was still trying to settle them down.

Spirit looked at the vast sky, picking out a bright star that he often saw sailing high over his home-land. He pulled in a deep breath, glad things were peaceful and quiet tonight.

Then a distant sparkle caught Spirit's eye and he turned to get a better look at it. It was flickering, like fire, but he knew it couldn't be fire.

When lightning hit trees in the forest, the flames

spread quickly. They spread even faster in the tall dry prairie grass.

Spirit shook his mane. The twinkling light had an orange-red cast. But it was tiny and it did not change, no matter how long he watched it. Had a star fallen to the earth somehow?

Spirit tilted his head, then turned back toward the herd. He caught his mother's eye, signaling for her to join him.

He gazed at the strange light until she was beside him. He switched his tail and looked at his mother, asking her to watch the herd until he could return.

She did not want him to go, he could tell, but she would take good care of the herd. He knew he could depend on her.

Spirit set off, determined to find out whether a star had fallen—or not. Whatever the strange new light in their homeland turned out to be, it was his responsibility to find out about it.

Chapter Three

*S*omething new had come upon the land that night—something that would change my life forever. And so my journey began.

Spirit traveled half the night.

The stars overhead glittered in silence in the dark arch of the sky. The breeze changed as the hours passed and Spirit could smell the unmistakable scent of fire . . . but the reddish glow did not spread, nor did it dim and go out.

As he got closer to the light, Spirit noticed another scent. He didn't recognize it. It was some kind of creature, but none that he had ever known.

Was it dangerous?

The young stallion slowed, staring, as he approached the strange glow.

It was a fire.

But it was small and round, and it was burning in a clearing where there were no trees. The sticks that were on fire were crisscrossed, stacked in a pile.

The creatures around it were funny looking, with odd, patchy coats. They were the source of the unfamiliar scent, Spirit realized.

They were all sitting much too close to the fire. Were they that foolish? Didn't they know that fire was dangerous?

Spirit edged closer. What kind of creatures could they be?

He watched as one of them walked away from the little fire.

It walked on two legs!

It looked impossible, but Spirit had to believe his own eyes. The creature did not fall down, though it looked like it ought to.

Spirit was fascinated. All the creatures were stretching now, finding places to sleep for the night. They spoke to one another, not whinnying, but making other kinds of sounds.

One of them bent over suddenly and appeared to be pulling off its own leg!

Spirit caught his breath.

This made even less sense than anything else he had seen. The creature did not seem to be in any pain as it tugged, hopping, to keep its balance. Then it stood straight again, holding something in its hand. Its foot, soft and long, did not seem wounded.

Spirit blinked, confused.

Its leg was fine, too, and still right where it ought to be.

It had pulled off something that had been *covering* its leg and foot.

Spirit shook his mane. Whatever the foot-and-leg covering was, the creature dropped it, then set to work pulling the same kind of covering off its other foot.

All the creatures went through this hopping-and-pulling routine before they lay down. Spirit wondered how they survived if their feet were so weak that they needed coverings. How could they graze or hunt or do whatever they did to feed themselves?

It wasn't long before the creatures stopped moving and making their strange sounds.

Spirit waited a little longer to be sure they were asleep, then stepped forward carefully, poised to run at the slightest sign of danger.

Halfway to the little fire, Spirit noticed a group of horses standing close around a single tree. The sight startled him.

Why hadn't he scented them?

What were they doing?

They had long vinelike things around their necks. Spirit was astounded. They were tied to the tree, he realized. They couldn't run, no matter what danger came. Spirit was amazed and confused by this. Why had they allowed the weak-footed creatures to tie them up like that?

He looked at them.

One of the horses gestured, whinnying quietly, urging him to run.

Spirit stamped a forehoof lightly. Imagine this

horse telling him what to do! It had been foolish enough to get itself tied to a tree. He was a lot smarter than that.

Spirit knew he was strong and fast. If any danger threatened him, he would gallop like the wind. But he wanted to find out what these strange creatures were first. He wanted to know why they had come to his homeland.

Spirit made his way slowly toward the sleeping creatures. None of them woke as he approached. In the firelight, he could see a pair of the foot-and-leg coverings standing side by side. Cautious but curious, he reached out, pushing his muzzle down inside to test the scent of the strange creature.

But when he lifted his head, the covering was stuck! It clung to his muzzle as he shook his head.

Desperate to escape the terrible smell inside it, Spirit shook his head harder—and the covering flew off. It sailed through the air and hit one of the sleeping creatures. It hit hard.

"Oof!" the creature said. "What the . . . ?" It moved, wrenching to one side.

"Ahhh!" another one answered.

It moved, too, and Spirit saw that it had the strange coverings on most parts of its body. He could see its skin only where the coverings left off. One thing was clear: These creatures had far too little fur to stay warm. They needed coverings for that, too.

"Oh man, look at that stallion," one of the creatures said quietly.

"It's beautiful!" another one added.

Spirit watched them a moment. They weren't getting up, and he was sure he could outrun them, so he approached one that hadn't awakened yet, and dropped his head low to sniff at its face.

"Sadie May," it mumbled. "Oh, mmmmmmm ... Sadie." Then it sighed deeply. "Quit it, Sadie."

Spirit touched the creature's cheek lightly, trying to understand its strange, furless skin.

The creature puckered up its lips and made an odd squelching sound. It pressed its mouth against Spirit's muzzle.

Spirit opened his eyes wide, amazed and puzzled.

"Ewwwww!!!!" two of the other creatures said. Then they made a loud, gasping sound, widening their mouths so that their teeth showed.

The sleeping creature suddenly woke, its eyes flying open. It made an alarmed sound and sat up. The rest of the creatures stumbled to their feet.

"C'mon, men!" one of them shouted.

Spirit wheeled around, startled. He hesitated, then broke into a canter. Men? Is that what they called themselves?

Shouts followed Spirit into the darkness.

"Look out! He's getting away! Get him!"

"Oh man, there he goes!"

"Come on, boys! Let's go!"

Spirit lifted his head and galloped faster. He had no idea what all the words meant, but the tone was clear enough. It was time to get away—far away. The men were coming after him.

Chapter Four

A wiser horse might have turned and run the moment he'd seen these strange creatures. But I wanted to know who these two-leggeds were. Many times later, I regretted my curiosity...

Spirit galloped with his head high.

He couldn't wait to show these two-leggeds how fast he was . . . He would leave them well behind, then get back to his post above the herd to keep watch.

Then he heard the sound of hoofbeats and glanced

back. What he saw nearly made him break stride.

The men had climbed up onto the horses' backs. And they were chasing him!

The idea of a man straddling his back, shouting and whooping, made Spirit grit his teeth. How could the horses stand it? Why would they allow it?

Spirit was confused, but he still wasn't worried. What horse could outrace him carrying a big, heavy, two-legged creature on its back?

Spirit galloped flat out for a little way, then dodged to one side, leaping into a deep ditch. He could hear the men and their horses passing at a gallop. The men were calling out to each other. The meaning was obvious. They were wondering where he had gone.

Spirit leaped up out of the ditch and charged after them, playfully biting one of the riders on the rear end.

The rider squealed and looked back, eyes wide. Then he lost his balance and fell from the galloping horse. He hit the ground hard and rolled.

Spirit made his way through the other horses,

bumping them aside, outrunning them easily. The riders tried to get their mounts to gallop fast enough to keep up, but Spirit pulled away, galloping hard. He kept up his burst of speed, and after a time he was alone with the sound of his own hoof-beats.

Spirit finally reached the ridge overlooking the herd and his heart lifted when he saw Esperanza and the others grazing peacefully—but then he noticed the sound of hoofbeats and voices behind him again. He glanced back. The men hadn't given up . . .

Spirit whinnied a warning to Esperanza. There were mares and foals that couldn't possibly get away from these men. Then he slid to a stop and pivoted to face his pursuers.

The rider shouted as Spirit lunged toward them, galloping past them, heading back in the opposite direction.

After a moment, the men managed to haul their horses around and were chasing Spirit again.

Tossing his head and squealing a challenge, Spirit

launched himself forward. He was stretching out, galloping faster and faster now. He was determined to outrun them this time—and to lead them away from the herd.

The countryside was open and there were few places to hide. When Spirit saw the mouth of a canyon, he veered off, jumping a wide ravine to get to it.

Pounding along the canyon floor, he glanced back. Only two of the riders had managed to follow him. He knew why. The other horses were afraid to jump that ravine.

Spirit dug in, and he began to distance himself from the riders. He could hear the men shouting to each other. The tone of their voices bothered him. They sounded happy.

"Ha ha! We got him now!" the first of the men hollered, whooping.

"You betcha," the second man shouted back.

At that instant, Spirit realized why they sounded cheerful. He had made a terrible mistake.

This was a box canyon.

The far end was closed by rock outcroppings.

There was no way out—except the way he had gotten in.

Spirit spotted an overhang and gathered himself, leaping upward, landing on a shelf of stone. Below him, the riders dragged their tired horses to a stop and looked up at him.

Without warning, Spirit leaped back down, nearly hitting the men. One of the riders launched himself out of his saddle, desperate to get out of the way. He hit the ground hard. The other one managed to haul on the reins, swerving his horse clear.

They shouted in their odd voices, short, sharp sounds.

"Whoa!"

"Look out!"

Spirit lunged past them once more and raced back toward the mouth of the canyon. He couldn't wait to be free of these creatures. He could see the wide, empty plains before him and he lengthened his stride.

Without any warning, one of the vinelike ropes

snaked out from behind him and looped over Spirit's neck. The feeling of having something around his neck terrified him.

In an instant, he figured out what had happened.

The other riders had caught up—and they had hidden to wait for him.

"Thought ya' got away, didn't ya, mustang?" a voice called as Spirit's speed nearly snapped the rope. He was yanked backward and fell, slamming into the ground.

Angry, Spirit struggled to stand.

He glanced upward and saw the herd on a rocky ridge, staring down at him. They must have heard the commotion and followed to help him.

He whinnied a furious warning when he saw Esperanza descending the steep hillside.

He did not want them coming any closer.

Esperanza obeyed reluctantly, leading the others out of sight. Spirit glanced at the men, relieved; none of them had looked up to spot the herd.

Looking back at the men, Spirit felt his anger rising. He hated the feel of the ropes around his neck.

He was scared, but not humbled. He would get away from these men, somehow; he had to. He glared at one of the riders' mounts. The horse turned away in shame.

Spirit knew the horses were not proud of catching him—but their riders certainly were. They were all sitting up straight, their heads high. They were *enjoying* his helplessness.

"We can sell him to the soldiers, I bet," one of them said. The others nodded.

Dragged along by the ropes, Spirit had no choice but to go with the riders. He had no idea where they were taking him . . . but it was far from his herd and his homeland. Every step added weight to Spirit's heart. Every jerk on the hated ropes hardened his resolve to escape.

The journey was long and miserable. Walking between two horses, with a rope halter tying him between them, Spirit was forced across high plateaus.

Crossing the Red Mesa, Spirit scuffed his hooves in the dry, rocky soil, but he had no choice but to keep going. When he tried to stop, the riders forced their horses to drag him forward.

Two days passed as Spirit shuffled along. The next morning he realized that he didn't recognize the countryside; it was outside his homeland.

Spirit felt a deep aching sorrow inside his heart. He had never been this far from the herd, from his mother and his friends. He had never left his homeland before. All he wanted was to go back to the herd. He missed them, and was worried about their safety.

The next morning, the men pulled Spirit toward a place so strange that he could only stare. It was surrounded by trees that had been cut and propped upright in a straight line, forming a high fence—something Spirit had never seen before. As they approached the fence, Spirit kept hearing them use the word *soldiers*.

Was this where the soldiers lived? What was a soldier?

The men who had caught him talked to men inside the fence for a long time. These men, Spirit understood, must be the soldiers. The soldiers handed his captors something that seemed to make them happy. It was small and Spirit couldn't see what it was before the men tucked it inside their skin coverings.

Then they got back on their horses and left.

The soldiers, too, wore body coverings over their furless skin. But theirs were all the same dark blue color. It made them look alike to Spirit. He couldn't imagine why they would do it. Surely their friends couldn't recognize them from a distance?

The soldiers grabbed the ropes that held Spirit and pulled him inside the wooden fort.

He felt rage building inside him again. It had been awful to be pulled through open country. But this was even worse. He longed to run free, to get away from this cramped, dangerous place. He had to find a way to escape.

Inside the barricade were more strange things.

There were tree trunks piled into tight little squares.

There were soldiers coming in and out of the

piles. The soldiers were *everywhere*. How many of them were there? Did they all live here? It was very confusing.

As Spirit was pulled forward, he saw that these men had captured other horses, too. They were standing uneasily, lined up and marching in straight rows, with riders on their backs.

"The army just bought a fine animal, Sergeant," one of the soldiers said to another.

Spirit stared at the lines of horses. One of them met his eyes with sympathy, only to be jerked back into the line by the soldier it was carrying.

Shaking, Spirit reared, unable to contain his fear and anger any longer. Somehow, the straight lines of horses were even more unnatural than the walls and the buildings.

Straining at the ropes, Spirit pulled the men along. They were shouting and angry and they leaned their weight against the ropes. But they couldn't stop him.

In a rage, Spirit dragged the soldiers forward. Straining, he managed to rear again and struck out with his forehooves. He would hurt them if he could.

Then they would drop the ropes and he would be able to escape and—

Suddenly a sound as loud as a thundercrack stopped him in his tracks. He dropped back to the ground and peered at the sky, confused. There was no storm.

Then Spirit looked up to see a man sitting astride a powerful gray horse. The man was holding something dark and shiny. Smoke rose from one end of it and Spirit understood at once that it had made the sound—and that it was dangerous.

Spirit saw instantly that this man was different from the others. He was tall and sat very straight in the saddle. His mane was longer than most of the rest. But that wasn't what set him apart. His eyes were full of a cold, fearless pride. He shook his head, his eyes fixed on Spirit.

"What seems to be the problem here, gentlemen?"

Two men answered his question at the same time.

"We got us a crazy one here, Colonel."

"Pure mustang, sir."

Spirit arched his neck, staring at the long-haired Colonel. The man met his eyes. Spirit saw that he had been right. There was no trace of fear in them. None. The Colonel raised a hand and the rest of the men quieted.

Spirit watched. Was this Colonel the leader here? All the others seemed to obey him. Spirit lowered his head and braced himself as the Colonel dismounted and began to walk toward him.

Chapter Five

We never questioned the ways of land and sky, no matter how sudden or cruel. We never asked why one of us didn't make it across the river in the time of high water. We never asked why a foal was born still in the grass. Nature had her reasons.

But this I didn't understand.

The Colonel jammed his riding whip beneath Spirit's jaw and forced him to lift his head.

"The army has dealt with wild horses before," he said. Then he turned toward the men who watched.

He gestured, pointing at Spirit with the whip. "This one will be no different."

Spirit wanted to attack. He wanted to break the ropes and lunge at the Colonel. But he knew he couldn't; the ropes were too tight, too strong.

But he could reach the hated whip.

Extending his neck, Spirit snatched it between his teeth, grinding at the leather. Then he jerked his head, snapping the whip in two, and flung it to the earth.

The soldiers holding the ropes glared at Spirit. One raised his hand in anger. But the Colonel just chuckled.

"Induct this animal, Sergeant."

One of the men stepped forward. "Yes, sir!"

Spirit fought the ropes, but it did no good. There were too many men and too many ropes. They dragged him forward and tied him to stout posts.

Then the sergeant shouted to one of the soldiers. "Murphy?"

"Yes, sir?"

"OK, he's all yours." The sergeant gestured at

Spirit. "Good luck. He's a wild 'un."

Murphy squared his broad shoulders. He was as wide as he was tall—and he looked fierce. "We'll see how wild he is when I'm done with him."

Spirit leaned forward and managed to get hold of Murphy's hand. He bit down hard.

"Ahhhh! Dagnabit!" Murphy exploded. "You want to fight, do you?"

The men strained at the ropes, tightening them around Spirit's belly, then wrapping them around two rails set deep into the ground.

"Right," one of them grunted. "Make sure that's good and tight."

"Tie him down good," Murphy shouted. Then he came forward again, his face set in a grim, angry expression. Spirit saw a flash of something shiny, then he felt an odd tugging at his neck. He strained against the ropes.

The tugging didn't hurt, but from the corner of his eye he could see long stands of dark hair lying in the dust. Murphy had cut off his mane!

Spirit wrenched around and snapped at Murphy's

hand. The man's shout told him his aim had been good.

Muttering, Murphy walked in circles, holding his injured hand. He whirled around and walked away—then came right back, carrying something Spirit didn't understand at first. Murphy shoved the contraption of leather straps onto Spirit's head and buckled it tightly. Spirit shook his head. The thing would not come off.

Even worse, the leather straps enclosed his muzzle completely. Spirit fought the ropes and tried to snap at Murphy again, but the leather kept his mouth firmly closed.

Spirit was furious, but he was also smart. He calmed himself and stood quietly, as though he had no more will to fight.

Nothing could have been further from the truth. He could no longer bite, and he could barely move, but he had other weapons . . . He would wait for a better chance to teach this man a lesson.

Murphy seemed to be fooled by his quiet stance as Spirit allowed him to approach carrying an armload of shiny objects. Murphy dropped the load heavily. Then there was a clinking sound as he picked up one of the items, an oddly curved thing. Suddenly, Murphy picked up Spirit's rear hoof and bent over it, raising a long-handled tool as if preparing to strike.

Spirit could barely believe what was happening. How could Murphy imagine for an instant that this kind of treatment would be allowed? What would he need something on his hoof for? Spirit turned his head just far enough to take accurate aim at Murphy's wide rear end. Then he unleashed a powerful kick.

Murphy was large, but Spirit's kick lifted him off his feet—and he fell heavily to the ground. Spirit raised his head proudly. A clear hoofprint showed on the back of Murphy's pants.

The horses in the stables and the corral—even the ones being ridden by soldiers—were all watching. And when Murphy hit the ground, they tossed their heads and whinnied with excitement.

Murphy stood up slowly. He was gritting his

teeth and scowling. He looked at Spirit, then walked heavily away. For an instant, Spirit thought he might have won, that the man would leave him alone now. Then he saw Murphy stop and bend over something.

Spirit could smell the soldier's sweat all around him. He could smell dust and hay and familiar horse-smells. But there was something else coming from the place where Murphy now stood—the scent of sharp, acrid smoke. A fire?

Out of the corner of his eye Spirit saw Murphy coming toward him again, carrying a straight rod that glowed red on one end.

Spirit didn't know what Murphy had in mind, but he didn't plan to wait and find out. He twisted, hard, kicking at the sergeant who stood close by. His hooves connected and he knocked the man flat. Then Spirit glanced at Murphy's angry face. This was it, Spirit knew; he had to win this battle once and for all. He lowered his head, glaring, gathering his strength and his courage.

"Murphy, look out," one of the men shouted.

But it was too late. Spirit ducked his head, lunging forward with all his strength. He butted Murphy hard, throwing him backward.

Murphy sprawled onto the ground. Spirit stood over him, his fury subsiding a little. The man didn't move. Good! For a few minutes, maybe, he wouldn't be dangerous.

A soldier was trying to speak over the shouts and confusion. "Uh, Corporal . . . " he began. "Round up some volunteers to, uh, take this animal to the stables."

Then the Colonel stepped forward again. This time, it was very clear that he was the leader. The Colonel's voice seemed to be like a herd stallion's call. The moment he spoke, all the men quieted and paid attention.

"Not the stables," the Colonel said evenly.

"Sir?" the sergeant asked.

The Colonel frowned angrily. "The corral. It's time to break that horse."

Spirit fought the ropes—but again, there were just too many men.

He struggled as the men threw a saddle on his back and tightened the cinch. The crushing pressure around his belly made him furious. The saddle pinched at his withers and he rippled his skin, trying to ease the pain, but he could not.

Never in his life had he been forced into doing *anything*. He had never questioned his freedom—or his right to stay free. Now he fought for every inch of ground they dragged him across, enraged at these soldiers, these men.

Shouting, they backed Spirit into a chute. The weight of a rider sank down onto his back and the saddle dug into his skin. It was an insult and a shock. Did they expect him to peacefully accept the burden like the horses they rode? He had been born to freedom. He would never give it up.

Without warning, the door of the chute opened.

Spirit's anger exploded. He rushed out, bucking, circling, wrenching himself forward, then back, twisting hard, kicking high with his hind legs, until the weight of the rider suddenly eased and was gone. A second later, the man hit the dust, hard.

He stood for a few seconds, breathing hard, then looked up, ready for the next enemy. It didn't take long. The men shouted to one another as they dragged him back into the chute.

"Get his head up now!"

"Hold him, watch it!"

Spirit lunged against the pressure of a second rider, slamming himself against the rails.

"Hup! No you don't!"

"Heeeea! Easy!"

Then the chute door opened. Spirit shot out, reeling and twisting, rearing high, then slamming back down, stiff-legged. The rider sailed off his back and through the air. When he hit the ground, Spirit heard him groan.

Getting up, the man glared at Spirit. "You lousy piece of horseflesh!"

Spirit could hear the insult in the tone of the man's voice. Arching his neck and clenching his teeth, Spirit turned slowly to face the man. Then he charged.

The downed rider ran toward the fence. "Get me

out of here", he shouted. "Get me out of here!"

A third rider headed toward the chute. Spirit glared at him, too. One thing was obvious. These two-leggeds didn't know when to leave something alone. The men crowded around him again, dragging him back.

Spirit came out fighting again. He threw the third rider, then a fourth, and a fifth, and a sixth. As the men hit the dirt, the cavalry horses whinnied and stamped their hooves, cheering him on.

Spirit galloped, charging the fence, determined to break through it and reclaim his freedom. But the stout rails forced him to a halt. In the billowing dust, while the other soldiers ran and scattered, he saw the long-haired Colonel standing still just outside the fence.

The Colonel was scowling, staring straight into Spirit's eyes. Spirit met his gaze and watched this hated enemy warily.

They stared at each other for a long moment. Spirit switched his tail back and forth, trembling with rage.

Finally, the Colonel lifted his eyes and shouted. "Tie this horse to the post. No food or water. Three days."

Spirit could tell something terrible was in store for him. He tried once more to fight the ropes that were tightening around him yet again, but every way he turned, more men appeared to drag him down, pulling him along by sheer force.

The post in the center of the corral was heavy and set solidly into the ground. Once the men had hitched the ropes around it and stepped back, Spirit tried to escape.

Spirit heaved his weight against the rope, over and over, then stood, breathing hard. He pawed at the dirt, flinging it up in chunks as he circled. Then he set his weight against the rope again and tried to break it once more. He could not.

The men watched him for a while, then began to drift off. By the time Spirit had exhausted himself, night was falling.

As the sun set he noticed a bright star high in the sky. It was one he had often noticed from the high bluffs in his homeland. He looked up at it.

This same star shone down upon his herd, Spirit knew. He pictured them, Esperanza and others standing watch, the colts sleeping safe. He gathered his courage. Somehow, he had to escape. He had to.

Chapter Six

*M*y heart galloped through the skies that night—back to my herd, where I belonged. I wondered if they missed me as much as I missed them.

Spirit waited out the long night. In the morning, the men in the fort woke and went about their chores. The sun rose and the day got hot.

Spirit was hungry, but it was his thirst that bothered him most. He shifted his weight and fidgeted, walking in circles around the post.

His hooves had worn a track in the loose dirt and the rope had worn sore places on his skin. He swallowed painfully and glanced up at the sun. It would get hotter still before it began to cool off.

Spirit noticed the long-haired Colonel staring at him. The man was taking a drink of water. Drops of the cool water ran down his chin and fell to the dusty ground.

Spirit met his eyes, swallowing painfully, longing for the cool clear lake of his homeland.

Just then a commotion at the fort gates made everyone look up. A group of soldiers came in, riding in close ranks with straight backs and set faces.

"We've got a hostile!" a soldier shouted.

Spirit glared at the rows of horses and their look-alike riders.

Abruptly, the rows parted and revealed the prisoner. He was a man—but he was gangly, not quite grown, like a three-year-old colt. His chest, back, and feet were bare—he wore fewer coverings on his body than the soldiers. His mane was longer than the Colonel's, and raven-wing black. He walked tall, his head high. His bearing had pride and strength and Spirit could tell he was also used to being free.

The man-colt walked with dignity as the soldiers brought him forward, even though they had tied his hands with rope and were leading him like one of their horses.

Spirit watched the Colonel.

He was scowling. "Well, what do we have here?"

The sergeant squared his shoulders. "We caught him by the supply wagons, sir!"

The soldiers held their captive still so the Colonel could look him over. The Colonel mumbled something to himself, then straightened. "Take the boy away, gentlemen. Show him our best." Spirit watched and listened. So the man-colt was a *boy*.

The sergeant saluted, then shouted, "Corporal, take the boy to the stockades."

The Colonel shook his head. "Not the stockades. The post." He paused, then frowned. "No food or water."

The boy was led past Spirit. Their eyes met and the boy gaped at Spirit. One of the soldiers slapped the back of his head. "What are you looking at, boy?"

Spirit glared at the soldier. These men were cruel for no reason. Why would men want to tie another man—and a man-colt at that—to a post? Were they going to try to saddle him, too? This made no sense.

The boy looked away from the soldiers, staring at the sky as they tied him to the post. Spirit watched, wondering if the boy wanted to escape as badly as he did.

"Hey," the boy said quietly to Spirit as the soldiers walked away. "I'm Little Creek." Then he made clicking and clucking sounds in his throat.

Spirit looked at him. Was the boy trying to tell him something? These sounds weren't like any of the others Spirit had heard the men making. Perhaps this boy was making fun of him? Spirit snorted.

Little Creek snorted back at him, a good imitation of Spirit's sound of disgust.

For a moment, Spirit just looked at him. Then, offended by what seemed like mockery, Spirit turned away from the boy, standing with his hindquarters squared in Little Creek's direction.

Since he could not walk away from this impudent man-colt, he'd just have to ignore him.

Late that night, when the soldiers were asleep and the fort had been silent for a long time, Little Creek began to hoot. He sounded exactly like an owl. Spirit watched him closely, wondering what in the world he was doing.

Was he hoping that an owl would come save him?

Spirit twitched his ears, listening. He heard something rustling outside the fence, a tiny whisper of a sound.

Then a wolf began howling from the same direction. Except it wasn't a wolf, he was sure. It was a man imitating a wolf's voice, just as Little Creek had imitated an owl.

This made even less sense than everything else.

If Little Creek's friends wanted to talk to him, why not use a language they could actually speak and understand?

A silver glint of light in the dark caught Spirit's

eye. Something shiny and sharp sailed downward, landing by Little Creek.

Little Creek slid his bare foot out, gripping it with his toes. He kicked, arching his back and jerking his leg up. The shiny thing flipped upward and the boy caught it in his teeth. Then, with a single shake of his head, he tossed it over his shoulder.

It landed neatly behind him, close to his bound hands. Spirit could see how sharp one end of it was. The other end was dull and darker—that was the end Little Creek had clutched with his toes. It was what he was fumbling to grasp with his hands now.

Little Creek had a determined frown on his face. Spirit waited, unsure what the boy was trying to do. It was nearly dawn. If he was trying to escape he had better hurry. The soldiers would soon be up.

Just then a blaring bugle startled Spirit into turning away from the boy. He looked at the buildings.

The soldiers were pouring out and lining up in that odd way they had. They stood quietly as the sergeant stepped in front of the long lines of troops. "C-Company. Ten-hut!"

The men straightened and stood rigidly. Spirit shook his mane and stretched as the sergeant went on shouting. He spotted the Colonel standing nearby and stared at him with hatred.

"With the Colonel's permission, sir. Incoming patrol reports hostiles headed north. The railroad has expressed concern, sir." The sergeant took a breath. "They've requested additional patrols."

The Colonel turned and looked at Spirit. He ignored the sergeant's announcement and frowned. Then he glanced up.

"How long has it been, Sergeant?"

The man looked startled. "Sir?"

The Colonel frowned again. "The mustang. How long has it been tied?"

"Three days, sir."

Then he took off his hat and pushed his long hair back from his face. "Good. Fetch my crop and spurs." He resettled his hat.

Once again the soldiers forced Spirit toward the chute. A saddle was thrown on him and cinched painfully tight. A cold metal bit was forced between his teeth. It hurt just as much as the saddle.

The Colonel mounted quickly, settling his weight into the saddle.

The soldiers gathered around to watch.

Spirit stood tensely, ready to prove to this man that he could not be ridden, that he was wild and proud—a stallion of the Cimarron herd.

The Colonel tensed, as if he could sense Spirit's determination. "You can break easy . . . or you can break hard, mustang!" the Colonel told him grimly.

Spirit waited, knowing that in a few seconds, the gate would fly open. He readied every muscle in his body. The instant the chute opened, the Colonel dug his heels into Spirit's sides, adding one more infuriating pain and startling him into action. Spirit burst out, bucking and twisting.

Spirit slammed against the fence rails, then whirled and fought his way across the corral in a series of body-wrenching leaps.

The Colonel clung to his back, dragging at the reins. The bit was clamped against Spirit's tongue, nearly gagging him. It hurt horribly and the pain fed Spirit's anger. He would do *anything* to get this hated man off his back.

Remembering his fight with the cougar, Spirit ducked his head and pitched forward into the same kind of dangerous roll.

But when he staggered upright, the Colonel was still astride him.

Stunned by the Colonel's ability to hang on, Spirit stood still, his sides heaving from the effort.

"You see, gentlemen," the Colonel said to the soldiers lined up against the fence. "Any horse can be broken." He paused, then leaned forward. "Move along, mustang." He dug his heels into Spirit's sides once more. Spirit took a step forward, then another. The Colonel's weight made the stiff frame of the saddle dig into his back. Still, he walked forward, controlling his fury.

Spirit met Little Creek's eyes. The soldiers' horses were staring, too, but when Spirit glanced at them, they looked away.

The Colonel was sitting straight in the saddle. "There are those in Washington who believe that the West will never be settled," he began.

Spirit hated the sound of his voice. He hated the feel of the man's weight on his back and the creaking of the saddle leather. He walked slowly, dragging in long breaths, gathering his strength as he followed the corral fence in a wide circle.

"And it is that manner of small thinking that would say this horse could never be broken. Discipline, time, and patience are the three great levelers," he added grimly. Then he looked down at Spirit. "Mustang—" the Colonel said, then without warning, he jabbed his boot heels into Spirit's sides again. The sudden pain startled Spirit into action.

Spirit jerked the reins free and charged forward, leaping blindly at the hated fence. He crashed into it, then slid along the rails. He felt the cinch catch on something, then break under the strain of his weight.

The saddle slid loose, and Spirit wrenched around to throw it off his back. He felt the Colonel fall forward. He ducked his head and bucked once more and the despised weight left his back.

A second later he was staring into the Colonel's eyes as the man swung helplessly, hanging on to the bridle to keep from falling beneath Spirit's hooves.

Furious and frantic to be free, Spirit heaved himself upward, using all his strength to rear, throwing the Colonel backward, out of the corral. Then he fell against the fence again. This time, it collapsed under his weight.

Exhausted and fighting to stand up, Spirit saw Little Creek staring at him. The boy's eyes were full of admiration.

A chorus of triumphant whinnies shook the fort as the soldiers' horses reared and bucked, thrilled by Spirit's victory over the Colonel. They hated the Colonel, too, Spirit realized. They knew how cruel he was. A lot of them had probably felt his whip and his boot heels just as Spirit had.

Spirit watched them, then glanced back at Little Creek. The admiration was still in his eyes, and it strengthened Spirit's courage.

"Soldier!" the Colonel was shouting. "Secure that horse!"

Spirit turned to see the Colonel striding toward him, holding the thing that made the terrifying thundercrack sound. Spirit's heart raced. Whatever this thing was, it was deadly dangerous—and the Colonel's face was full of hatred.

Before Spirit could react, he was astonished to see Little Creek leap to his feet—suddenly free! In that instant, Spirit understood the sharp shiny thing. Little Creek had used it to cut through the ropes he could not reach with his own teeth. The boy raced toward the Colonel, throwing himself forward. The impact knocked the Colonel down.

Then Little Creek scrambled to his feet and began racing toward Spirit. The boy leaped, throwing his arms around his neck. Spirit shied, lunging into a gallop as the fort erupted into confusion around them.

Soldiers were shouting; there were so many voices that it sounded like the roar of storm wind.

The other horses were rearing and bucking crazily. The soldiers struggled to control them and the shouting grew even louder.

The Colonel was raging, screaming orders into the din.

As Spirit raced forward, his stride was lopsided,

awkward, with Little Creek's weight pulling him to one side, but he did not stop. He galloped, the boy struggling to hang on to his mane.

Passing a hitching post, Spirit knocked it flat, releasing the horses that were tied there.

Little Creek freed one hand from Spirit's mane and reached out. In one swift motion he managed to grab a soldier's rifle and fired the weapon at the stable doors. The shot blew them open and the horses inside rushed out, whinnying and jostling one another as they began to gallop.

Leading a thundering charge of freed horses, with Little Creek still clinging to his neck, Spirit veered, heading toward the front gates. Murphy tried to cut them off, but Spirit lowered his head and shoved the heavyset man aside.

Then the way was finally clear! Spirit plunged onward, lowering his head, desperate to free himself. He burst through the gates. With Little Creek still clinging to his mane, Spirit galloped onto the open plains, the cavalry horses strung out behind him, scattering in all directions.

With Little Creek whooping and yelling in celebration, Spirit outran them all.

As they pounded along, Spirit was glad Little Creek did not try to actually ride him. The boy clung to his neck and mane, without daring to touch the bridle reins or to straddle Spirit's back. Maybe he knew that Spirit would never have allowed it ... that their flight together would have become another battle instead.

Spirit pounded over the grassy land, exhilarated. He would get the bridle off somehow, as soon as he was far, far away from the soldiers.

Then he would never allow another two-legged to put ropes or straps on him, or to shove a metal bit in his mouth. He'd leave these men and their forts and their saddles far behind. He'd go home, to the freedom and the homeland that he loved.

Chapter Seven

I wasn't sure what had happened back there and I wasn't about to stop and ask. All I knew was that I was headed home...

Evening was deepening into dusk. Spirit knew he would have to stop soon, to rest somewhere for the night. Then in the morning he would leave alone. Little Creek could make his way back to his own homeland by himself.

Spirit couldn't wait to see his herd. As he ran, Spirit imagined them grazing quietly, then hearing his approaching hoofbeats. They would look up and turn and...

Little Creek whistled, startling Spirit. An instant later there were real hoofbeats. Spirit was amazed to see a beautiful pinto mare, running free, swinging in to gallop beside him. He felt Little Creek's weight on his neck increase, then disappear.

Spirit glanced at the horse beside him. Little Creek was settling himself on her back.

"Rain!" Spirit heard Little Creek saying. "I knew you would come."

Spirit looked at the mare more carefully, slowing a little. Her mane was long, part white and part brown, and her stride nearly matched his own.

Suddenly, Rain leaped forward, turning, forcing Spirit to slow. Was she playing? Her mane flared out and he saw that she had a long bird's feather tangled in it.

A second later Spirit felt ropes drop around his neck. Two young men about Little Creek's age had appeared from nowhere.

Spirit felt his heart sinking. More ropes!

Spirit tried to free himself, but the ropes held fast and he didn't fight them for long.

He knew he would never allow himself to be ridden or tamed. But he hadn't eaten or had water in three days and the hard battle with the Colonel and the long gallop had sapped his strength. He was too tired to resist these new captors.

Little Creek and his friends escorted Spirit to a place even stranger than the soldiers' fort. The beautiful pinto mare showed no fear and Spirit knew it must be familiar to her.

It was another settlement of men. But there was no tall fence around the shelters here. And the shelters themselves were much different from the straight, square structures where the soldiers lived.

These were all curves and slopes, shaped like fluted flowers, round at the bottom and tapering to a narrow opening at the top. Pine poles stuck out of the tops, like the sticks of an eagle's nest.

Like the fort, it was instantly clear that men lived here. Their smells and their odd-sounding voices were everywhere. But unlike the men at the fort, these men had families.

Everywhere, Spirit saw more man-colts. Some were long-legged. Some were older, while others could barely walk. The little ones had high, piping voices.

As night fell, Little Creek and the others led him to a corral and turned him into it, then closed the gate carefully.

Spirit looked at the gate, the fence rails. They looked strong—too strong to break. And they were too high to jump.

"Steady," Little Creek was saying gently. He reached up to slide the bridle carefully over Spirit's ears.

Lowering it slowly, he eased the bit from Spirit's bruised, sore mouth, his voice gentle. "Nice and easy. There you go," he said. "There, that feels better, doesn't it?"

Spirit looked at the boy.

It was wonderful to have the hated bar of metal out of his mouth. Spirit realized something; not all men were alike. Little Creek was not cruel. The Colonel would not have cared if Spirit's mouth ached.

Spirit lowered his head, feeling the exhaustion of the long day. He barely noticed when the boys left him alone in the corral.

The next morning brought a surprise. A pile of apples was stacked in the corral.

Spirit moved toward them, intrigued by the sweet scent of the fruit. He lowered his head and began to eat, enchanted by the incredible taste.

Then he noticed Rain standing across the meadow, watching him.

He raised his head.

She had looked pretty by moonlight, but the morning sun made her even more beautiful. Their eyes met and he tossed his head, neighing to her.

Just then, Little Creek appeared, calling out to Rain. Spirit watched, astounded, as the mare answered, then cantered to meet him, treating the boy as though he were one of their kind. And the scrawny, two-legged boy pranced around her like a love-struck yearling!

Spirit snorted in disapproval. Rain and Little

Creek were playing! It was ridiculous!

Not long after that, Little Creek came to the corral without Rain. His two friends climbed to the top rail to watch as he came through the gate, carrying a blanket. Spirit watched him warily.

"Great Mustang," Little Creek said respectfully, "today I will ride you." Spirit blew out a breath, understanding the boy's intent. Surely Little Creek didn't imagine he would allow this?

Little Creek came toward him with the blanket. Spirit sidestepped him and cantered in a tight circle.

Little Creek tried again. Once more, Spirit whirled and moved away. The boys on the fence laughed. Little Creek glared at them, then started over.

For a long time, they danced back and forth. Little Creek was gentle and patient. Spirit was equally patient—but not quite as gentle. He planned to avoid the boy until he gave up. Spirit liked Little Creek in a way, and he didn't want to end up hurting him, but he refused to let himself be ridden.

But Little Creek would not give up. He was persistent, just like the other two-leggeds had been. He kept circling, holding the blanket carefully, talking in a soft voice.

Spirit cantered in endless circles in the little corral, then, finally, his impatience exploded. He charged Little Creek. The boy ran to dive between the corral rails, sprawling on the ground just outside the fence.

Spirit lowered his head, whinnying a fierce warning.

Suddenly, Rain appeared, her ears pinned back in protective fury. To Spirit's amazement, she didn't run—she didn't even seem to be afraid. Instead, she whinnied a challenge right back at him.

Spirit was stunned. Few mares would stand up to an infuriated stallion like this. And he could not imagine why she would protect a man-colt. But he admired her courage, even if he couldn't understand it. He stepped back from the fence.

Rain and Little Creek left together and Spirit watched them go, puzzled and uneasy. He hated the fence that stopped him from going where he wanted to go. And he missed the herd terribly; like any horse, he didn't like being alone.

The next time he came, Little Creek let Rain into the corral with Spirit. Spirit was surprised and delighted. His loneliness was becoming hard to bear and this strange, brave mare intrigued him.

He watched Rain as she sidled through the gate and moved gracefully into the corral. He stood close to her, ignoring Little Creek as the boy circled them, talking softly.

"Okay, Rain," the boy said, a little louder. "Let's see if you can teach this mustang some manners."

There was a light touch, then something slid around Spirit's neck. A rope! But before he had time to react, the boy was opening the gate!

Spirit did not hesitate.

He bolted toward freedom. But he had only galloped a few strides before he felt a heavy pull at his neck. Forced to slow, glancing back, he blinked in amazement. The boy had tied the other end of the rope around Rain's neck.

They were hitched together!

Spirit surged forward, dragging Rain along. Once they were out of the corral, he galloped with heavy, lunging strides, trying to make her keep up.

Rain let him pull her along through the village. They passed the odd-shaped shelters.

They passed people.

One family had a toddling baby who gazed up at Spirit with a toothless smile on her round face.

But when they left the village and Spirit tried to gallop toward open country, Rain reacted. She set her weight and pulled him to a stop.

Spirit threw himself against the rope, but Rain leaned back, refusing to budge. He waited a few seconds, then sprang forward again, hoping to catch her off guard.

It didn't work.

Glancing back, he saw the mare sitting on her haunches, a stubborn look on her face.

Spirit stood still, furious, his sides heaving. He was so close to freedom. How could she keep him from it? And why wouldn't she want to be free herself?

Rain got up slowly. Switching her tail in grand, graceful arcs, she began to walk toward him. Passing so close that her mane brushed his muzzle, she circled him. Spirit's anger subsided as he turned his head to watch her. She was so pretty, so calm.

Then, without warning, Rain sprang to the side, pulling the long rope tight around Spirit's legs. For a second, he struggled to keep his balance. But he couldn't, and he thudded to the ground heavily.

Rain stood watching him as he slowly stood up. He glared at her, seeing the shine of amusement in her eyes. He shook his mane angrily. It wasn't funny.

Her eyes still twinkling, Rain set off, her step even and deliberate.

Spirit balked, then followed, the tether between them making it impossible to refuse without starting another argument. He wasn't sure he wanted to cross this stubborn mare again. It didn't seem to do him much good.

Rain led him down by the river, then into the village with its odd, slant-sided shelters. The people they passed looked fondly at Rain. The same tooth-less child they had seen before smiled and laughed as they came back.

She wandered in front of them. Rain stopped and sniffed at her carefully. It was obvious the baby knew Rain well and was not afraid of her size or her strength.

Curious, Spirit lowered his head.

To his amazement, the child showed no fear of him at all. Instead, she reached up and took hold of his muzzle, pulling his nostrils wide. It tickled. Spirit snorted, startling the child so that she fell backward and started crying.

Spirit looked at her. He hadn't meant to hurt her or scare her. He lowered his head, meaning to touch her gently with his muzzle, to let her know he was sorry.

But the child reached up and wrapped her arms around him. Her tiny hands pressed against the sides of his face.

Uneasy with the human-foal clinging so tightly, Spirit lifted his head just enough so that her feet swung free of the ground. Then he lowered her back down, hoping she would let go.

She did. Then she toddled off. "Bye, bye, horsey," she said as she went. Her voice was as tiny as she was—and as gentle.

Chapter Eight

I guess it's safe to say that I had never met anyone like Rain before. And I had never seen a place like her village. I knew that leaving would be hard for her and that she would be scared, but more than anything I wanted to share my homeland with her.

Spirit followed Rain throughout the settlement where Little Creek and his people lived. These two-leggeds seemed to have more respect for other creatures than the soldiers did. They built very few fences and their horses were allowed to roam much of the time. They hunted only when they were hungry. They were very careful of their fires.

It was clear that Rain cared deeply for Little Creek. He had knotted the feather into Rain's mane. Spirit could tell she was proud of it.

Spirit was not at ease with these men and all he wanted was to gallop away, back to his own herd and freedom. But the truth was, he didn't want to leave alone. And he would have followed Rain almost anywhere that morning.

Rain led Spirit toward Little Creek and his friends. Spirit stared at them. They were marking their horses with blue paint! Spirit watched, bewildered, as one of the young men carefully drew a blue circle around a horse's eye. Spirit tensed, astonished. Why didn't the horse buck or run?

Then Little Creek turned, reaching up to make a blue mark on Spirit. Spirit tossed his head. He didn't want to be painted! Aiming carefully, he kicked at the paint bowl, splashing it all over Little Creek. He snorted as the boy wiped the thick blue liquid from his eyes.

Spirit expected Little Creek to be angry—but he wasn't.

The boy's eyes were sparkling. He was smiling. Spirit could only toss his head. He would never understand these two-leggeds.

Walking with Rain beyond the village, Spirit noticed her looking at an apple hanging high in a tree.

He reared, rising on his hind legs to grab it between his teeth.

Stretching out his neck, he offered it to Rain.

She looked at him—admiring his strength and grace—then lowered her head to graze. Spirit placed the apple in the grass near her, then lifted it again, meeting Rain's eyes as she raised her head.

He had gotten it for her. He wanted her to have it. After a moment, she understood.

Spirit held very still as Rain leaned closer to take half the apple he held between his teeth, her lips brushing his muzzle.

After they shared the apple, they walked on. The day was warm, and it got hot by midday. To cool off, the horses waded into a wide, still pond. The water streamed around them, water lilies bobbing in their wake.

Spirit watched Rain as she swam. He wondered if she could possibly like him as much as he liked her. Or was she merely putting up with his company because Little Creek's tether held them together?

Just as he thought it, she turned and met his eyes. Everything he needed to know was in her gaze. She liked him very much. Spirit's heart rose.

Wading out of the water, they walked close together as he led her up a ridge. At the top, he took his old protective stance, searching the horizons for enemies. Overhead, an eagle soared, crying out in its wind-whistle voice.

Spirit called back, but the bird didn't seem to hear him. It sailed onward, out of sight.

Spirit looked at Rain. For the first time in his life, he felt torn two ways.

He longed to go home.

But he did not want to leave Rain.

He followed her back to the corral with confusion in his heart.

The next day, Little Creek tried to ride Spirit again. And the next. It turned into a kind of game between them, an excuse to leap and gallop, to dodge and swerve. Finally, Spirit let Little Creek mount. But then he threw him to the ground.

Still, Little Creek didn't give up.

He kept getting on, only to have Spirit buck him off over and over again.

One morning, when Little Creek's friends laughed at his attempts to ride Spirit, Spirit got angry with them.

He chased them off. He wanted to protect Little Creek from their jokes. He would never allow the boy to ride him—but he did like him. And he could tell the laughter hurt Little Creek's pride.

Another morning, Little Creek surprised Spirit. "I'm never going to ride you, am I?" he muttered as they dodged around the corral. He straightened up and sighed. "And no one ever should."

Then, without warning, the boy strode toward the corral gate and lowered the rails. He motioned at Spirit. "You can go. It's okay—go!"

Spirit waited, alert and uneasy. Was this a trick?

Would he be roped again if he tried to run?

"Go on," the boy repeated. "Get out of here! Go home."

Spirit hesitated a second longer, then bolted past Little Creek, galloping hard. But he didn't head homeward. He veered off, determined to find Rain.

He knew it would be hard for her to leave, but he wanted more than anything to show her the joys of a free life, to have her become part of the herd he loved.

When he found Rain, Spirit gestured for her to follow. He could tell that she wanted to. He could tell that she also wanted to stay. She took a few steps with him, then stopped and looked back toward the village.

Spirit waited, his neck arched, tense, as she tried to make her decision. He stamped a forehoof nervously. He had to leave before anything happened to stop him. This was the moment he had waited for—but he didn't want to leave without her ...

A sudden faint sound of hoofbeats made Spirit turn. Rain lifted her head and pricked her ears.

There were many horses, and they were headed toward the village.

Galloping together, Spirit and Rain climbed a ridge and saw a terrible sight. The Colonel was coming, riding at the head of a long line of galloping horses. He shouted something and soldiers turned their horses toward the village.

Spirit and Rain watched, stunned and helpless, as the soldiers attacked. The people of the village rushed to defend themselves.

Frantic, whinnying, Rain galloped back and charged into the thick of the battle, looking for Little Creek. Spirit followed and tried to stay close to her, intent on protecting her from the soldiers' guns and swords.

But the chaos of the attack separated them and Spirit whirled around to find her gone. He galloped on, frantically trying to find her again in the confusion. All around him, the loud sounds of shouting and gunfire shattered the usual peacefulness of the village.

When Spirit finally spotted Rain on the riverbank, she was in the worst kind of danger. She was galloping flat out, carrying Little Creek in a furious charge, straight toward the Colonel himself.

The Colonel raised his gun to fire at Little Creek.

Rain reared in terror and the bullet intended for Little Creek struck her shoulder instead. Spirit's heart plummeted as the mare reeled back from the bullet, falling sideways into the rushing water.

Little Creek was thrown off her back. As the boy clung to a rock in the strong current, the Colonel was staring at Spirit. Then he turned to Little Creek and raised his gun again.

Spirit lunged forward, racing toward the Colonel. At the last possible instant, he shouldered the Colonel's horse hard enough to make it stagger just as the gun went off. The shot went wild and the Colonel fell.

Through the noise and confusion Little Creek was looking at Spirit. The mustang had just saved his life.

Spirit wasn't thinking about his enemy, or the

boy he had come to care about. He was looking downstream.

The current was lifting Rain, carrying her away. Spirit whinnied frantically and followed, galloping along the shore. He glanced back at the Colonel and saw a look of astonishment on the man's face—as though he had seen something he couldn't believe.

The Colonel watched for a moment as Little Creek released the rock he clung to and floated with the current to escape downriver. Then the Colonel reset his hat and looked around for his own horse. He had no time to wonder about a mustang. There was a battle to fight.

Galloping hard to keep up with Rain's progress down the river, Spirit heard the sounds of the battle soften and fade behind him.

As the river's current roughened, turning into rapids, he leaped from the bank into the river and swam after Rain. He fought the swirling current. He could see Rain in the choppy water ahead of him. He neighed frantically, but she did not answer.

Finally, as the river rounded a wide bend, he

managed to get close to the mare. Her eyes were open. She was alive! Spirit's heart soared as she turned sideways in the swift water. He positioned himself so that she could lay her head on his back, using his strength to keep her head above the fierce current.

The water was too deep to find footing on the rocky bottom, so Spirit fell into a strong swimming rhythm, supporting Rain, pulling her along. Spirit's heart was rising.

Rain was alive. They would be all right. He would find a place where the current was slower, the banks less steep, a place where he could guide Rain out of the water. She needed to rest . . .

A rushing roar in the distance caught his attention. He knew what it was instantly, but he didn't want to believe it. A waterfall!

As the current shoved them along, he struggled to swim. He needed to tow Rain into the shallow water, to get them both out of the river. But he couldn't. There wasn't enough time and the current was too swift.

As the river whipped them around a bend, the roaring sound rose to a deafening thunder.

Spirit fought to save himself and Rain, but the current was stronger than a thousand horses and it swept them onward and over the falls.

The drop was dizzying. Spirit fought his terror and tried to stay in sight of Rain, but the cold water closed over his head as he fell.

When he hit the pool below the falls, he seemed to go downward forever, sinking helplessly in the roiling current.

Fighting for his life, he swam for the surface, bursting into the air just as he was feeling like he would never breathe again.

Spirit twisted in the water, looking in every direction. Where was Rain?

Finally, he saw her.

Thrashing in the water, fighting the current, he made his way out of the river to stand beside her where she lay on the bank.

She was breathing.

Barely.

Spirit stood over her, willing her to open her eyes, but she didn't. Her strength seemed to be utterly gone, as though she had given up.

Spirit lay down beside Rain, moving as close as he could to keep her warm, to let her know that he was there. Finally, she lifted her head and rested her muzzle on his shoulder.

Spirit listened to Rain's faint, fragile breath. He willed her to live. He was determined to protect her no matter how long it took for her to regain her strength.

"Hey, there are a couple of horses down here!"

Spirit tensed at the sound of a voice on the slope above them. He glanced upward. Soldiers!

His instincts screamed at him to get up, to gallop away. But he refused to leave Rain's side, even when he saw the ropes the soldiers carried.

"Leave the mare," one of them said as they came close. "She's not going to make it."

Spirit fought the men, but he was too exhausted, and as always, there were too many ropes. The soldiers dragged him away. He whinnied frantically at

Rain and she lifted her head a little to answer, but her voice was so weak it terrified him. He struggled, but the ropes held him fast.

Calling sadly to Rain, Spirit could only stumble along, going where the soldiers forced him to go.

Spirit did not see Little Creek emerge from the trees and run to Rain's side. Spirit couldn't hear Little Creek's voice when the boy looked after him and spoke.

"You saved my life," Little Creek said, watching Spirit disappear into the forest, once again a prisoner of the soldiers' ropes.

Chapter Nine

*E*ven though all the love I had was left by the river that day, I knew I had to be strong for my herd. And for Rain.

Spirit was cold. He was scared. The men had forced him to walk, without rest, for a long time. They had finally stopped in this noisy, bustling place.

There were many men shouting, working, loading wagons, and coming and going through the falling snow. Spirit couldn't make sense out of any of it.

He had never seen anything like the huge metal contraption that puffed and snorted billows of steam and foul smoke.

He had heard the name that the men called it.

It was a *train*.

The men were very proud of it, he could tell. He couldn't see why. It stank and it hurt his ears. It ran only in a straight line, following metal tracks that the men had laid down for it.

When Spirit understood that the soldiers were trying to lead him *toward* the train, he fought the rope. So did some of the other horses that had been captured from Little Creek's village. But it did no good.

Shoved inside the railroad car, Spirit hung his head. The other horses kept glancing at him, glad he was there. He saw eagerness on their faces and he knew why.

They had seen him walking free with Rain. They knew he had never been ridden, that he was wild and had once led his own herd. They were hoping he would lead them to freedom. But how could he? He was as trapped and helpless as they were.

Spirit moved away from the other horses as the train began to roll forward. What was the point in being brave now? Everything he cared about was gone. He would probably never see his herd again.

Or Rain . . .

He let out a long breath. It hurt too much to think about Rain lying on the riverbank, too weak to move.

Spirit shivered.

As the train picked up speed, the wind got stronger, driving the swirling snow through the slats. His eyes and lungs stung from the thick, sharp-smelling smoke of the engine.

Turning his back on the other horses, Spirit stared out between the slats and watched the snow falling.

The flakes whirled and blurred against the dark sky. As Spirit watched, his heart heavy, the flakes seemed to form shapes.

He squinted against the cold and the wind. The patterns in the blowing snow reminded him of galloping horses—for an instant it was as though he could see his own beloved herd, racing through the storm.

Spirit watched the swirling snow, imagining the sound of the herd's hooves. He could almost see his mother galloping in the lead. He pulled in a long breath and his heart lifted.

He was not alone.

His homeland and the Cimarron herd lived inside him.

He had to be brave so that one day he could return to them. All he wanted was to take his post on a bluff above the herd, to protect them and lead them again.

Spirit lifted his head and pulled in another long breath of the icy air. He glanced at the other horses, then turned toward them. They stood uneasily in the swaying train car.

Spirit was sure that they were afraid, too, that their hearts were as heavy as his own. He moved to stand close to them, taking comfort in their nearness and trying to keep his head and spirits high enough to give them comfort as well.

But it was not easy. The motion of the train made him feel a little sick. The noise of the train was frightening. But he kept pulling in long breaths. Finally he dozed a little.

When the train stopped and the door rolled open, Spirit looked out and was astonished at what he saw. They had arrived someplace similar to the fort, but bigger, and with many different kinds of men. They all seemed to be intent on whatever work they were doing.

Spirit could hear shouts and a ringing sound. Men were striking at the slick, hard metal the train and its rails were made from.

"Come on," a man was saying gently to Spirit. "It'll be all right. That's it."

Spirit knew better than to trust the man's reassuring tone of voice. But he allowed himself to be led down the ramp, looking at the scene around him.

It seemed as if these men were trying to kill the earth. Everywhere, the grass had been trampled flat.

The trees had been slaughtered and piled in two long, endless stacks that ran up the slope above him. The soil itself had been gouged and scraped.

And the noise of the men's voices and machines drowned out the silence of the sky, the song of the birds.

Spirit had no idea why he had been brought to this place. He only knew that he had to find some way to get back to his homeland. He thought about the herd again and tried to keep his heart from sinking in sorrow.

A sudden volley of shouts made Spirit lift his head. A distant booming sound made him flinch. It echoed off the trees, then faded slowly.

Spirit blinked. It had been louder than any gunshot, any crashing strike of lightning. Every man in the settlement turned to face a distant mountainside, already scarred by huge, ragged holes.

A group of soldiers rode past.

Spirit scanned their faces, afraid he would see the Colonel among them, but he did not.

"Well, that's it," a man standing near Spirit and

the other captured horses said. "We're hauling the steam engine up the mountain."

Beside him, a man wearing a black hat shook his head. "That's crazy."

The first man frowned. "We've got six days to connect with Utah. We move out at dawn."

Spirit warily followed the man who led him to a corral. The sun set, followed by a long, tense night. Standing close to the horses from Rain's village, Spirit managed to sleep a little just before dawn.

At sunrise, dried grass was thrown into the corral and the horses circled it to eat.

Spirit ate—not because he had an appetite for this brittle, lifeless grass, but because he knew he would need all his strength to escape.

He kept glancing up at the men who walked past the corral. There were so many of them here. And he knew they couldn't be trusted. It made him uneasy just to look at them.

Far from the railroad town, Little Creek was all alone.

He was walking the strangest path he had ever seen—the path made for the steam-belching train engine and the cars it pulled.

Men had laid squared timbers upon the earth, close together, in what seemed to be an endless line. Running on top of the timbers were two rails of the metal men called steel.

Neither rail wavered from its position—the distance between them stayed the same as far as Little Creek could see.

Why would men build things like this?

The straightness of the rails seemed out of place in this land of curving hills and sloping valleys.

Little Creek's face was set and grim as he walked.

He had seen Spirit being forced into the train and he knew that if he followed these rails long enough, he would find the proud mustang stallion.

He just hoped that he would find him unhurt and unbroken—with his heart and his pride still strong.

Chapter Ten

My journey had somehow brought me to a place where man had destroyed the land itself. I didn't know why the trail led here. What I did know was that I had to find a way to escape.

It took hours for the men to get all the horses hitched to the massive wooden sled they had built. On top of the cumbersome sled was the steam engine.

Spirit heard the word repeated over and over as the

men bustled around the horses, fastening buckles, adjusting chains. The steam engine had to be moved upward. The steam engine would make their work easier.

Spirit started. The steam engine looked bigger and heavier than any pile of boulders he had ever seen. It was long and black and it jutted out in weird shapes and angles that only men would think to build.

The horses were hitched together in pairs. There were two long lines of them, standing side by side.

Standing uneasily in one of the front ranks, Spirit kept glancing back down the slope.

He had never seen this many horses in one place. They were of every color, every size, some old and some young, all yoked together by the heavy harness chains. They all looked scared.

Spirit thought about what it would take to free himself from the harness.

The straps were thick and sturdy. The metal chains were stout. The lock-and-pin system that held the harnesses to the sled was strong. It would have to be if they were going to drag the enormous steam locomotive.

Some of the horses were thin and looked worn down, Spirit saw. Maybe they had been in this settlement a long time and were being worked too hard. It seemed likely.

Spirit looked uphill. A wide passage had been cleared between the sled and the top of the slope.

The forest had been cut and the fallen trees dragged out of the way, left in an impassable jumble on either side of the cleared trail. The ground was rough and steep and would make uncertain footing for them as they went.

Men moved along the ranks of horses. Many carried whips. They all looked grim-faced and determined.

"Ready to go!" a man standing on the great wooden sled cried out.

Whips cracked and a round of shouts went up from the men. Startled, Spirit leaned into the harness and struggled to move forward.

It seemed impossible.

The horses around him were groaning with effort and still the enormous sled did not move. He glanced back, past the straining horses and the shouting men. The locomotive stood like a dark cliff behind them.

A whip cracked close by and Spirit faced front. Alert, watching the horses around him, he threw his weight into the harness again.

The chains clanked and rattled as the horses fought to pull the engine uphill. Finally, it moved, a tiny jerking motion that made the straining horses stagger forward.

A weak-looking mare hitched close to Spirit faltered. A man noticed and brandished his whip. Spirit lunged, snapping viciously at him.

Were these men that stupid? Hitting a weak mare would not make her stronger.

The man backed off and Spirit concentrated on pulling—not because the men wanted him to, but because the weaker horses needed help.

Inch by painful inch, the horses dragged the engine upward. The slope was steep and uneven.

Behind the sled, men drove spikes into the ground to prop its weight up when the horses had to rest.

The whole day passed in straining and pulling and the sound of cracking whips. Spirit staggered along, his great strength challenged by the ordeal. He began to feel the despair he had felt on the train rising inside him again.

Then, finally, as the sun was hanging low in the sky, they reached the ridge and saw the hills beyond. He heard a shout.

"We're almost at the top! Slow down at the front!"

The whips drove them on a few more steps, then they were allowed to stop at last.

Spirit looked over the crest of the ridge and blinked.

A distant range of mountains formed a semi-circle of peaks. Spirit stared. There were red-rock canyons between him and the mountains and a river flowed in wide curves. The sun sparkled off a distant lake, sending up silvery flashes of light.

Spirit's heart rose. He knew those mountains. He

knew almost every path that led through the canyons.

The land that spread out before him was his homeland.

He had wanted so much to show it to Rain, to share it with her. A deep longing filled him, then a single thought made him catch his breath.

This railroad was heading straight toward his homeland. These men would capture the horses and force them to work beneath whips and chains. They would cut the ancient trees and scar the earth itself—just as they had done here.

Spirit knew he couldn't let it happen.

Frantic, he glanced around. The harness chains were too strong to break. The wooden blocks that held the lock-and-pin fasteners were too far to reach.

Suddenly, Spirit got an idea.

He closed his eyes and staggered. Then he fell to the ground and lay still.

The horses around him watched with worried eyes. Men gathered, talking in low voices. One of them nudged Spirit with the toe of his boot. Spirit held himself perfectly still. He forced himself not to react.

The man stepped back. "Get the mules up here!"

Grunting with effort, the men wrapped a chain around Spirit's legs and unhitched him from the rows of exhausted horses.

Spirit forced himself to lie limp as the mules dragged him off to the side of the cleared path, then started downhill. Then, just as he was dragged even with the sled, Spirit exploded into action.

The men who had thought him close to death leaped backward to get out of his way as he kicked off the chain wrapped around his legs and stood up.

Spirit galloped back toward the sled. The horses lifted their heads, startled. He slid to a halt and turned to kick apart the pins and locks that held the harnesses.

He whinnied in triumph. When the wood shattered, one of the long lines of horses was freed from the weight of the engine!

Spirit whinnied again, frantically, urging the horses to run. They realized what had happened

and shook off their weariness to stampede, scattering up over the ridge as Spirit kicked at the second
set of locks and pins. As he freed the second line
of horses, men ran toward him, shouting, their faces
twisted with anger.

The sled, without the horses' strength to hold it,
began to slide. It jerked backward an inch at a time.
The great engine on top of the sled began to sway.
The lumber in the sled groaned under the strain, the
uneven slope forcing it to turn as it went.

The men panicked, shouting, trying to circle
Spirit. They managed to get a chain around his
neck, but he reared, yanking it out of their hands.

The instant he was free, Spirit leaped away from
them and raced around to the downhill side of the
sled to avoid being caught again.

Then he looked up and his heart almost stopped.
The angle of the slope had tilted the sled sideways
and the engine was rocking back and forth. Spirit
leaped forward, terrified as it fell, crashing to earth,
sliding, its great weight rolling it over—right toward
Spirit.

Spirit galloped for his life as the engine slid behind him in heavy jerks down the slope, then hit a swale and rolled over again.

Its momentum kept it moving, crashing downward, grinding over the scarred earth, crushing rocks with its massive weight. Spirit galloped hard, barely managing to stay ahead of it.

The slope got steeper and the engine picked up speed. Spirit stretched out, thundering over the ground, racing for his very life.

Chapter Eleven

I had known that was when I had to stop pulling—and start fighting, like I never had before.

And now I knew I had gallop, faster than I ever had before . . . or I would never see my homeland again.

The massive engine jolted and crashed behind Spirit, shaking the ground as it came down the mountain.

The wide path that had been cleared in the forest had become a trap with the fallen trees piled into tall stacks like fences on either side. Because of the stacked trees blocking the way to safety, he could not escape the path of the steamer that thundered down the mountain behind him. He could only hope to outrun it.

Spirit galloped flat out, the chain still around his neck, flying behind him.

The tearing screams of bending steel filled the air, broken only by the booming thuds that shuddered through the soil when the train was thrown into the air by swells and hillocks—then came down again, bruising the very earth.

Spirit's breathing became a desperate gasping as he charged onward. He could feel vibrations from the huge locomotive through the earth beneath his hooves and it terrified him.

Suddenly, the vibration and the noise stopped and he could hear the sound of his own hoofbeats.

Puzzled, Spirit glanced backward and didn't see the sliding engine. For a second he was relieved. Then he realized what it meant.

The engine had bounced into the air. Spirit

stretched out, forcing his aching legs to pump faster as he fought to gallop out from beneath the shadow of the falling train.

The eerie instant of silence ended with a terrifying crash just behind him, so close that Spirit felt a stinging spray of pebbles and dirt as the massive steam engine gouged the mountainside.

The train had landed inches from his back hooves, the force of its impact throwing it back into the air. Spirit galloped faster than he ever had in his life. The engine hit again, spewing up dust and gravel. But Spirit had gained a little bit of a lead.

He began to hope. He could see the village ahead, the noisy town of two-leggeds where the other train had brought him yesterday. Spirit plunged downward. He charged straight at a planked building at the foot of the slope. The roar of the crashing engine shook the very air as he galloped through the wood-framed doorway. A window on the far side shattered as he leaped through it to keep going.

He lunged past a group of workers, startling them into leaping out of his way. Their faces went rigid as they looked past him and saw what was chasing him.

Then, just ahead, Spirit saw another engine, as big and heavy as the one that was sliding down the slope behind him. He veered toward it.

Making a desperate leap, Spirit clattered upward, scrambling onto the engine. Galloping along the top, he leaped off just as the falling engine slammed into it.

The crash threw sparks in every direction.

As he galloped clear, Spirit slowed, then stopped. His breath heaving and his legs shaking, he turned to look back.

The silence was eerie.

He trembled, afraid the train would somehow waken and begin to chase him again. But it did not. He shook his mane. He pawed at the dirt and took a few steps. The dangling chain snaked along the ground behind him.

In that instant, an explosion shook the valley. Flames and smoke billowed outward, rising into the sky.

With sparks falling around him like red-gold

snow, Spirit whirled and burst back into a gallop.

The pine forest erupted into flames as sparks landed in the dry timber, and the fire spread fast.

Spirit saw rabbits and deer as he galloped. Every creature in the forest was running from the murderous heat and choking on the smoke.

He headed toward the river by instinct, leaping high to clear a fallen tree. The chain around his neck trailed out behind him, dragging over the branches of the tree.

Just as Spirit's forehooves touched ground, the chain caught on the jutting stub of a broken limb.

Spirit's weight and momentum pulled the chain tight, jerking him to a halt. Terrified, he swung sideways, feeling the deadly tightness of the chain around his throat. Then he dropped to the ground, the chain so tight he could not breathe.

The heat of the fire was terrible, the roar of the flames just as fierce. It stung at Spirit's skin as he tried frantically to draw a breath. He fought the chain, but he could not break it or yank it free—it only tightened around his throat.

Spirit despaired. After everything, was he going

to die here, in a fire made by men? He thought of his herd. Then he remembered Rain lying on the riverbank. She had faced her death bravely. He could do no less.

Suddenly, a blur of motion caught Spirit's eye. A man was running toward him, silhouetted against the flames.

No, Spirit realized, not a man—a *man-colt*.

It was Little Creek!

Spirit saw the boy leap astride the fallen tree to beat at the limb stub, shattering it to free the chain.

Spirit dragged in a deep breath as it loosened. But he was so weak with exhaustion that he could not rise. Little Creek dropped down beside him, coaxing him, refusing to let him give up. Spirit struggled upright and together they ran.

The fire became two high walls, closing in on them.

Racing along side by side, they managed to outrun the inferno, but not by much. Then, suddenly, their path ended at the edge of a river gorge.

They could not hesitate.

The blistering heat of the fire left them no choice.

Together they leaped in the air and plummeted downward. For a terrifying second they hung in the air, then they plunged into the icy water.

The water was deep. The coolness closed over Spirit's head and he felt a rush of joy. This water meant life and escape and Spirit welcomed both with all his heart.

When he surfaced he saw Little Creek swimming for the far shore. Spirit followed him. With weak, shaking legs they staggered from the water together. Grateful to Little Creek, overwhelmed with exhaustion, he sank to the soft sand beside the river and closed his eyes.

Chapter Twelve

I didn't know where Little Creek had come from or how he got there—but I had never been as happy to see anyone in my whole life. I realized I owed my life to this two-legged.

The next morning, Spirit woke to see a pile of apples near him on the riverbank. He scrambled upright and looked down toward the water.

Little Creek was in the shallows, bending over to drink.

It seemed like a lifetime had passed since they had been together in the corral, running and dodging as

Little Creek tried to ride him. Spirit realized that he had missed the game. He had been scared and angry for so long that he felt like he'd forgotten how to play.

Careful to walk silently, Spirit slowly made his way up behind Little Creek.

Then, without warning, Spirit nudged him, jumping back as Little Creek fell face first into the clear water of the river.

The boy sputtered as he stood upright and saw Spirit staring down at him. Then he pretended to frown angrily, an exaggerated, silly expression. Little Creek ran at Spirit and the two of them leaped and sparred, splashing in the water.

When they finally gave up the game, Little Creek smiled. "I knew I would find you," he said, lifting his hand to touch Spirit's neck in friendship.

A faint sound startled Spirit. Abruptly, he turned to look back at the bluff they'd leaped off the night before.

Cavalrymen!

Spirit narrowed his eyes. It was the Colonel! The

long-haired soldier looked as surprised to see Little Creek and Spirit as they were to see him. Spirit felt his blood rising as he remembered every insult and cruelty, the bruising pain of the saddle. Then he pictured Rain, lying helpless and alone on the river-bank. He glared at the Colonel, barely able to keep from attacking him.

A soldier raised his rifle.

Little Creek shouted at Spirit. "Go! Go! Hah! Get out of here!"

They ran at the same instant. Then, without warning, Little Creek fell, sprawling onto the dirt.

For a few strides, Spirit galloped on, then slowed. The sound of cantering hooves told him that the cavalrymen had skirted the bluff and were quickly approaching.

Rain had loved Little Creek, Spirit knew. And the man-colt had saved his life.

Spirit made a sudden decision that he knew might cost him his own life. As he turned to gallop back, he realized that being forced to carry a rider was different from choosing to save a friend.

Stretching out, slowing a little, Spirit lowered his head so that Little Creek could grasp his mane and swing up onto his back. Then he whirled and pounded away again.

The Colonel and his men rode hard, whipping their horses. But Little Creek rode lightly and Spirit managed to stay ahead.

The soldiers didn't give up. The Colonel led the way, his eyes full of anger and determination, one hand on his rifle.

Spirit veered, heading for the mouth of a canyon, staying close to the river as it thinned and got shallower.

The red-rock cliffs and spires made it difficult to see far ahead. Spirit galloped on, hoping that the soldiers would lose sight of him. The ground was rocky and it was dangerous to keep up a flat-out gallop, but he did. He waited for the sound of hoofbeats behind him to dim.

Once they had, he turned again.

In the distance, Spirit could still hear the Colonel shouting orders.

"Split up! Split up!"

The Colonel sounded angry. The next time he glanced back there was only one man behind him, riding hard, leaning forward over his horse's neck.

Spirit veered into a narrow red-rock branch canyon. Little Creek bent to pull a dead limb off a tree as they clattered past, then he turned around to ride backward.

As they passed beneath a natural arch, Little Creek jammed the stick into place, ducking beneath it.

A few seconds later the stick caught the soldier across the chest and he fell from his horse.

Spirit veered onto a path that rose curving to the right. It looked narrow and rocky. He was sure he could outrun the cavalry mounts in such rough country.

The trail spiraled upward and Spirit lunged with every stride, determined to get away before the other soldiers came to help the one Little Creek's trick had unhorsed.

Gaining ground on the upward slope, Spirit drew away, racing around a tight corner only to skid to a stop where the path seemed to end.

He was high above the canyon floor now, about halfway up the red-rock spire.

Hoofbeats behind him made him whirl around.

Another rider was galloping toward them. And he was coming fast.

Spirit glanced around. The path did continue, off to one side! He picked up speed, Little Creek sitting forward to help his balance. He stayed close to the spire. The trail here was dangerously narrow.

The soldier whipped his horse into a frantic gallop and managed to catch up just long enough to shove viciously at Little Creek.

The boy slid sideways.

He gripped Spirit's mane as he fell, then hung, his feet swinging out over the sheer drop-off as Spirit leaned into a turn.

Heading into the next tight corner, Little Creek fought to hold on as the soldier came up alongside again.

Spirit galloped faster, forced to the outside of the curving path as the soldier leaned out, trying to knock Little Creek into thin air. Spirit could see over the edge. The canyon floor was even farther below them now.

Little Creek swung his weight forward, then back, then managed to vault himself upward, kicking the soldier hard. Spirit held steady, keeping his stride and his balance as the soldier lost his seat and fell onto the rocky path behind his horse. He shouted furiously as Spirit and Little Creek galloped onward, leaving him behind as they clattered up the trail.

A sharp turn in the path brought Spirit to another sliding halt. He blinked. One more stride and he would have fallen. His front hooves were poised on the edge of a steep drop. He heard loose pebbles fall downward. Little Creek let out a breath and Spirit knew what he was thinking. Another few inches and they'd have plunged downward.

Spirit looked around. This time the path did not go on. But there was a rough incline. There was no other option. He climbed it, placing his hooves carefully.

At the top, Spirit found himself standing on a pinnacle, a flat surface of red rock bounded on every side by nothing more than thin air—and a hundred-foot drop. They were trapped. There was no way out.

"There they are!" came a shout. "Up there!"

Spirit looked downward. The Colonel and two soldiers were glaring up at them, their faces stony with anger. A shot rang out and the bullet whistled through the air close to Spirit.

He turned and stared at the far rim of the canyon.

It was far from them—too far.

Spirit narrowed his eyes.

Or maybe not.

He might make it ... if he jumped with every bit of his strength, with luck, with the wind to help, with all the hope of freedom in his heart ...

Spirit lifted his head.

He refused to give up, so close to his homeland.

The boy had traveled a long way to find him—and he had saved Spirit's life.

The hoofbeats were getting louder. In seconds, the Colonel and his men would be upon them. Spirit tensed his muscles, then backed up until his hooves were balanced on the far edge of the pinnacle, his tail hanging over the sheer drop.

A pebble clattered, rolling, then fell.

Spirit fixed his eyes on the far rim of the canyon.

"Oh, no," Little Creek murmured, realizing what Spirit intended to do. But he centered his weight and Spirit knew he would ride light as a feather.

Lunging into a gallop, Spirit drove his hooves into the rock, gaining speed with every stride.

Never taking his eyes from the far rim, he galloped across the pinnacle.

Then he leaped outward with all his strength and all his will.

Sailing into the open air, Spirit kept his neck extended and his hooves poised.

On Spirit's back, Little Creek straightened, lifting his arms like spread wings, whooping with the sheer joy of flying.

Spirit's mane and tail fanned out, riding the wind

like wings as he passed above the chasm of the canyon. Far below, the sparkle of the river reflected sunlight back into the sky.

Then the ground on the far side seemed to rush up at Spirit, and the impact when they hit jolted through his body. He went down hard and Little Creek spilled forward, sliding on the rocky ground.

For a long moment they both lay still, gasping for breath, their eyes closed.

Spirit felt heavy, as though the reckless flight of the jump had taken his strength away and left him only the will to keep breathing, to drag in one long breath after another.

Finally, Little Creek stirred and sat up.

Spirit opened his eyes.

Little Creek's face was full of joy, like a newborn colt seeing the sky for the first time.

Spirit met his gaze and tucked his forelegs beneath him, heaving himself upright. Together they stood, swaying on their feet, looking back at the impossibly wide chasm they had leaped.

The Colonel and two soldiers were sitting on

their horses on the far side, staring in disbelief.

One of the soldiers lifted his rifle.

Spirit glanced over at Little Creek, then looked around.

The canyon rim was bare sandstone, without a single tree. It was flat and wide. There was nowhere to run, nowhere to hide.

The soldier cocked the rifle. He raised it to take aim.

Then the Colonel reached out to push the rifle barrel downward. The soldier lowered his gun.

The Colonel met Spirit's eyes and he nodded, his head moving slightly, a gesture so small the other soldiers didn't seem to notice it.

Spirit lowered his muzzle slightly, imitating the man's gesture, understanding it perfectly. It was a signal of truce, of respect. The battle between them was over.

Abruptly the Colonel pulled his horse around in a circle and rode away. The soldiers followed.

Little Creek whooped, a joyous shout. Spirit reared, prancing in a circle while Little Creek jumped up and down, shouting, celebrating. For a moment they were lost in the sheer happiness of being alive.

Then Spirit looked at Little Creek. He moved closer to the boy, offering to carry him once more—after all, they were making the same journey, he was sure. They both wanted to go home.

Little Creek hesitated, then swung up. The two friends started off together.

Chapter Thirteen

I had discovered more than just what lay beyond the Red Mesa. I had learned that we are shaped by our journeys, forged by our pain, strengthened by the beauty and kindness we might find along the way.

Spirit cantered, covering the ground, eager to return to his homeland, to find the Cimarron herd. First, though, he would return Little Creek to his village.

After a time, following the scent of campfires and the river, Spirit saw the pole-topped lodges. He felt Little Creek lean forward and he cantered faster, understanding the boy's eagerness.

Plunging to a halt on a bluff overlooking the village, Spirit waited for Little Creek to slide off his back. He could not stop himself from looking down at the village, remembering Rain.

He lowered his head, caught by the sorrow he had not allowed himself to feel fully—until now. She had been brave and graceful, and her heart had been true. Spirit missed her so much; he felt the loneliness like a wound.

Abruptly, Little Creek raised his fingers to his lips and blew, making a sound not unlike an eagle's call. Spirit wondered what it meant. Then he heard hoofbeats.

Looking toward the village, he was astounded to see Rain galloping toward them. He thought for a moment that he was seeing what he wished he could see. But the pinto mare galloping toward him was very much alive.

Spirit felt as though the earth had changed around him, as though the sunshine were brighter, warmer, the sky a deeper blue. He sprang into a gallop and raced to meet her.

They came close, sliding to a stop, facing each other. Then they both reared, dancing on their hind legs, whinnying joyously as they celebrated together.

For a long moment, Spirit and Rain stood close. He touched her face with his muzzle and he could smell sweet apples on her breath. She nuzzled his neck and he felt a weight leave his heart.

Then it returned.

One thing hadn't changed.

He wanted to go back to his homeland. Rain might not want to leave Little Creek and her own home.

He glanced at Little Creek. The boy was smiling as he walked toward them. He was looking at Rain.

"You will be in my heart always," Little Creek told her. He reached up and took the feather from her mane, loosening the braid until it fell free.

Then he faced Spirit. "Take care of her, Spirit-Who-Could-Not-Be-Broken." Little Creek put his arms around Spirit's neck. "I'll miss you, my friend."

Spirit backed away from the boy slowly, meeting his eyes for a long moment. Men were different from horses, but this was a farewell, he was sure. Little Creek had said good-bye to him and to Rain. The feather had marked her as Little Creek's own horse. But Little Creek had taken it back. Rain belonged to no one but herself now.

Spirit glanced at Rain. Love shone from her eyes and he knew she had already made her decision. The feather in Little Creek's hand meant that he understood and was happy for her.

They were free to go.

Spirit turned, Rain at his side.

He whinnied a farewell and Rain echoed it.

Then, together, they cantered across the grassland, the sky wide and blue above them. They played at times, bucking and rearing, but always coming back to run side by side.

They came to the river and passed beneath the cottonwood trees, the shadows dappling their coats.

A familiar call sounded overhead and Spirit looked up to see the eagle swooping downward. She leveled out and flew with them, swooping over their heads, then angled upward, slowing and rising to let them catch up.

Spirit and Rain cantered to a knoll that over-looked his homeland and stopped. The eagle sailed past them, crying out once more.

Below them, Spirit saw the Cimarron herd. The colts had all grown—the pair he had saved from the cougar were tall and leggy now. Then he spotted his mother. Esperanza was standing a little apart, keep-ing watch for enemies.

Spirit tossed his head and reared, then sprang into a gallop. Whinnying excitedly, with Rain at his side, he galloped toward the herd. The horses, startled, looked up from their grazing. They recog-nized him and answered his whinnies.

Esperanza came forward, her eyes shining. Spirit reared, and for a moment, they bucked and reared, overjoyed to see each other.

The news of Spirit's return spread through the herd and the other horses began to celebrate, too. They reared, tossing their heads.

Spirit and Rain led them in a gallop across the wide valley of his homeland, their hooves rolling like thunder, their hearts joined in their shared love of freedom.

And far above the herd, the clouds seemed to gather themselves into shapes that echoed the silhouettes of the horses themselves. Spirit's heart soared as high as the eagle that circled overhead. He was home.

I had grown stronger and wiser. I had learned that the Wild West is more than just a place. It's what we carry inside—no matter where our journey takes us. It is our spirit . . .

And some spirits can never be broken.